They All Ran Away

Written by Eleanor Spencer

Illustrated by Andrew Stephens

Three little bugs
came out to play.

A spider came out
and they all ran away.

Three little spiders
came out to play.

A mouse came out
and they all ran away.

Three little mice
came out to play.

A cat came out
and they all ran away.

Three little cats
came out to play.

A dog came out
and they all ran away.

Three little dogs
came out to play.

A big dog came out,
and . . .

. . . they all ran away.